Strange ... But True?

GHOSTS

ELIZABETH NOLL

BLACK
RABBIT
BOOKS

Bolt is published by Black Rabbit Books
P.O. Box 3263, Mankato, Minnesota, 56002.
www.blackrabbitbooks.com
Copyright © 2017 Black Rabbit Books

Design and Production by Michael Sellner
Photo Research by Rhonda Milbrett

Library of Congress Control Number: 2015954852

HC ISBN: 978-1-68072-024-2   PB ISBN: 978-1-68072-293-2

Printed in the United States at CG Book Printers,
North Mankato, Minnesota, 56003. PO #1795 4/16

Image Credits
Adobe Stock: artefacti, 6 (top);
Alamy: Dale O'Dell, 9, 24, 27; nage-
lestock.com, 4–5; Getty: Hulton Archive
/ Handout, 6 (bottom); istock: gmnicholas,
10; kentarcajuan, 3; Shutterstock: Antlio, Cover;
donatas1205, 20 (bottom right); Fer Gregory,
31; FoodStocker, 13 (top); Hollygraphic, 16–17;
jordeangjelovik, 13 (bottom); Leszek Czerwonka,
1, 32; Peter Dedeurwaerder, 20 (top); SDL, Cover
(bottom left), Back Cover, 22 (background), 28, ; SJ
Travel Photo and Video, 19; Valentyna7, 12 (left);
vitalez, 14; watin inthapan, 12 (right)
Every effort has been made to contact copyright holders for material reproduced in this
book. Any omissions will be rectified
in subsequent printings if notice is
given to the publisher.

Contents

CHAPTER 1

A Headless

Ghost

A guard stood quietly outside a palace in England. Suddenly, a white **figure** began walking toward him. He looked for her head. There was nothing there!

The guard yelled at the figure to stop. But the headless woman kept coming. The guard charged her with a knife. But the knife passed right through.

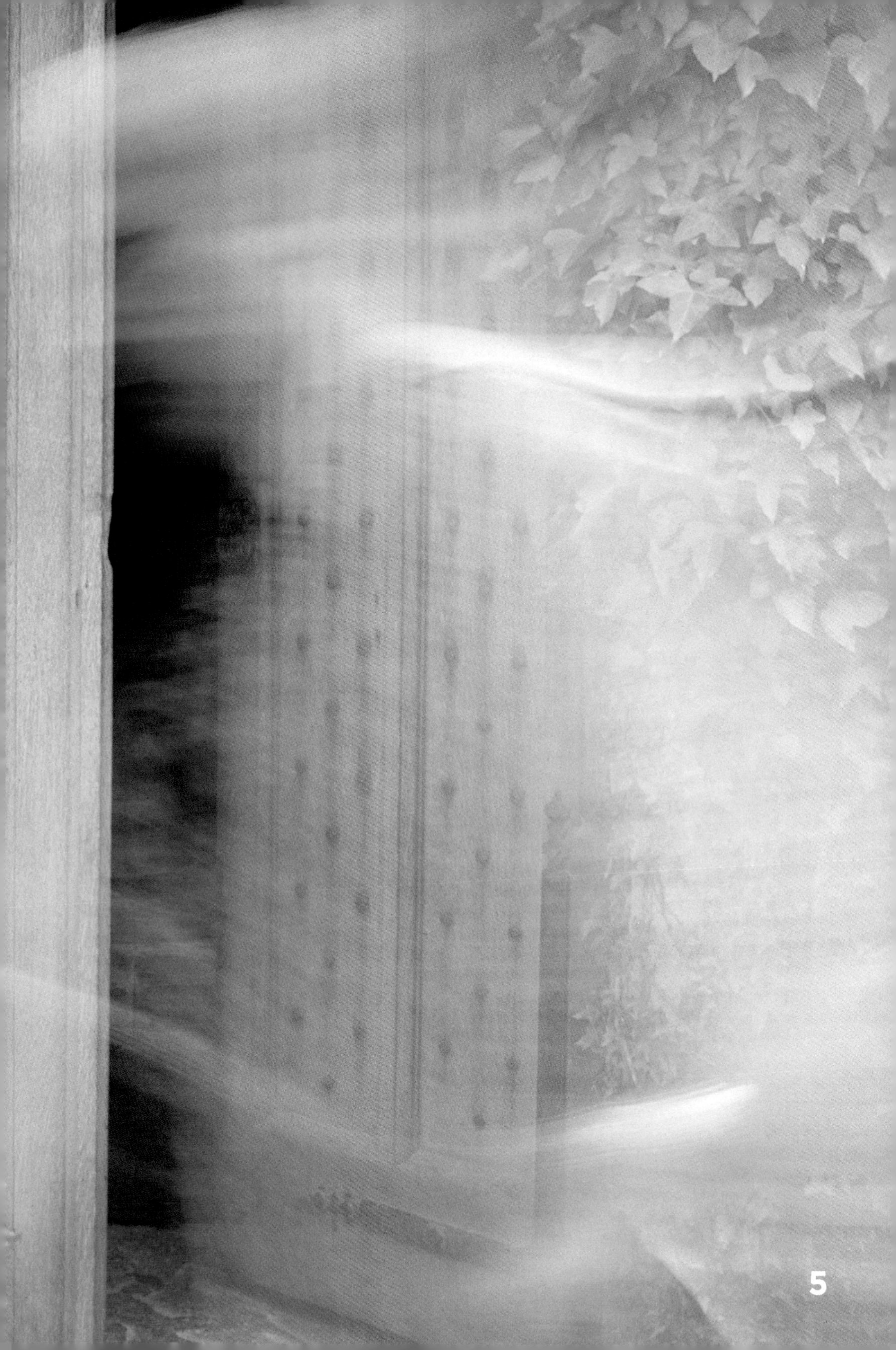

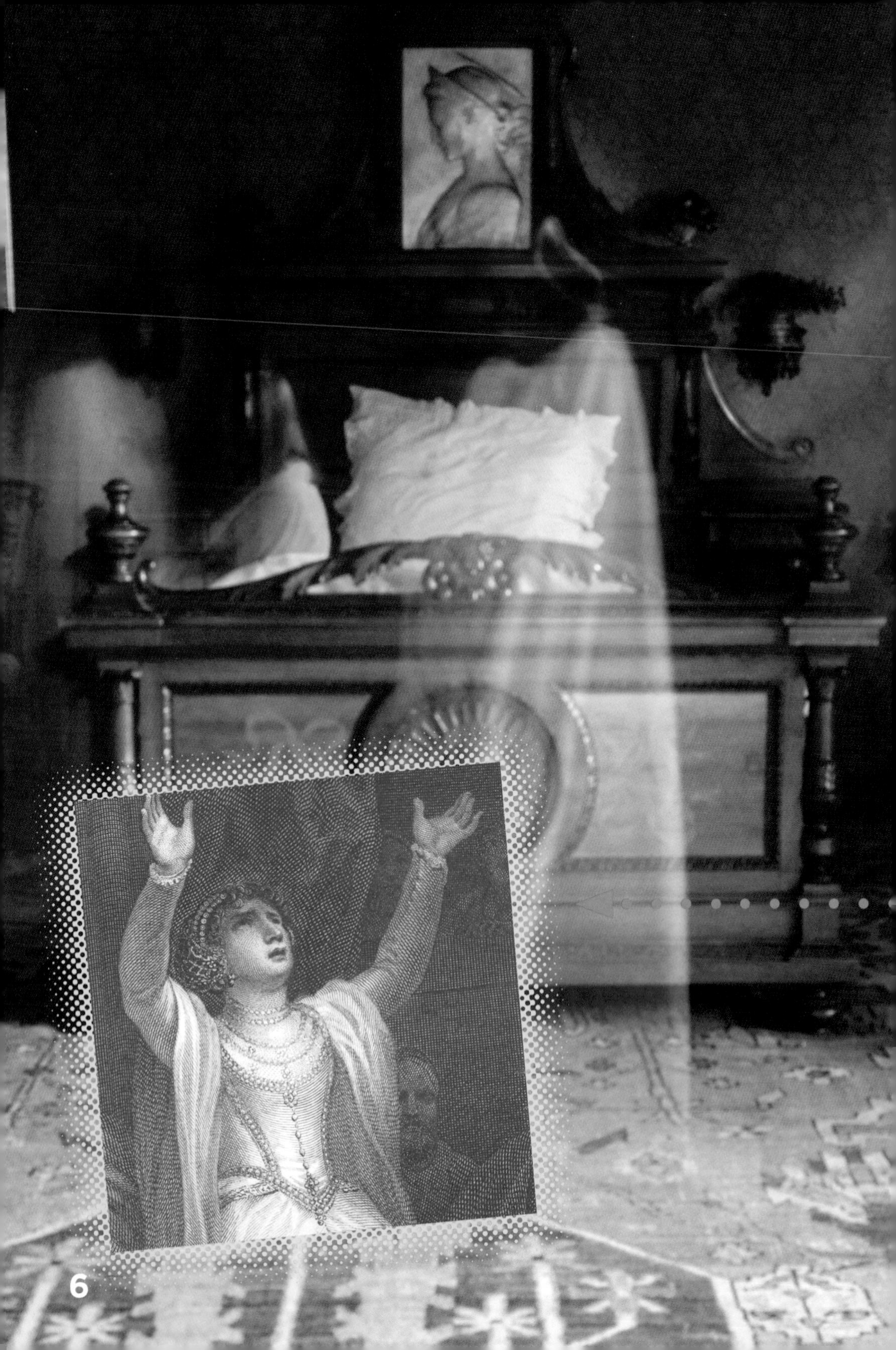

Spooky Ghosts

The guard claimed he had seen the ghost of Anne Boleyn. His story is just one of thousands of ghost stories. Ghost stories have been around for hundreds of years. But no one knows for sure if ghosts are real or **imagined**.

Anne Boleyn was married to King Henry VIII of England. The king had Anne's head cut off in 1536. Some think she **haunts** places because of her cruel death.

CHAPTER 2

Seeing

Stories say ghosts come in many forms. And they act differently too. Some stories say ghosts look like real people. Others describe figures that are see-through or like bright lights.

Stories talk about ghosts that open and close doors. Some people have even reported seeing ghosts throw objects. But other stories describe ghosts that float by quietly.

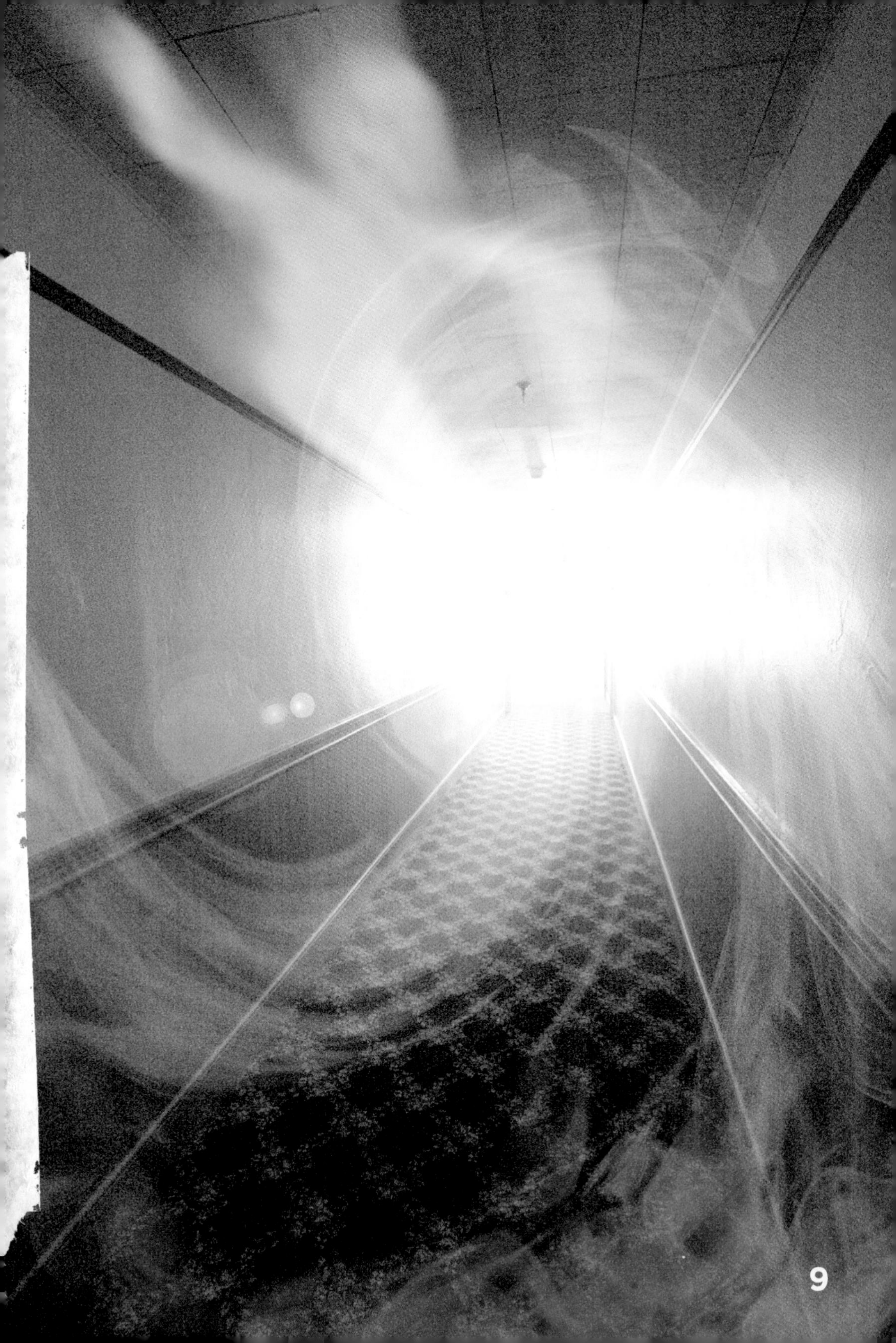

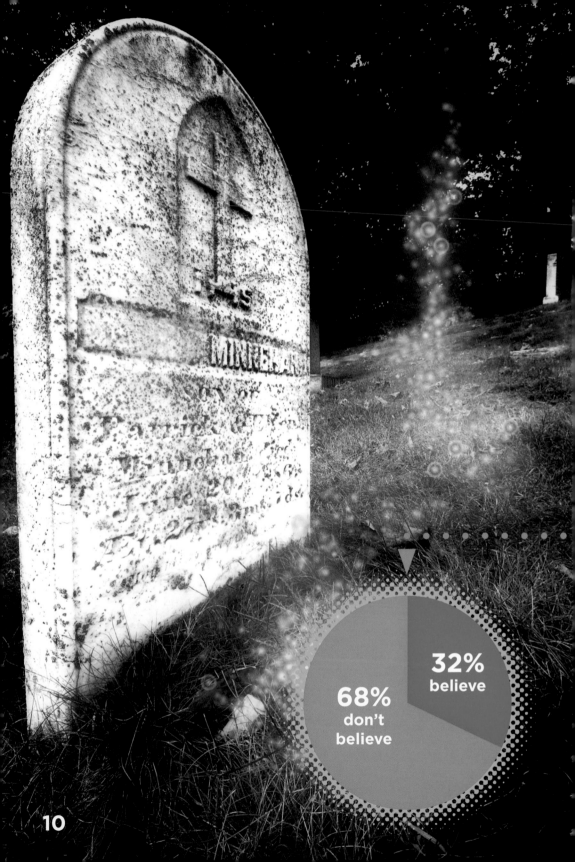

32%
believe

68%
don't
believe

Where Ghosts Are

People say ghosts haunt places where they lived. Ghosts might also stay where they died. Stories of ghosts are common in **cemeteries**, old hotels, and prisons.

How Many Believe?

Less than half of Americans believe in ghosts.

Ghost Hunters

Ghost hunters are people who look for **evidence** of ghosts. They go into places that are thought to be haunted. They listen for strange sounds. They also feel for cold air and watch for odd spots of light.

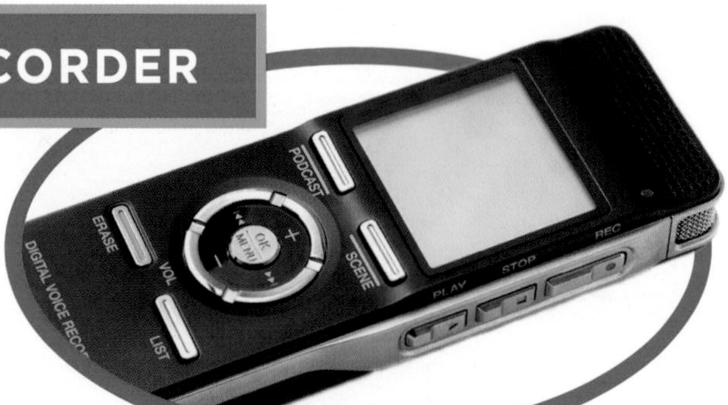
PODCAST
ERASE
VOL
SCENE
LIST
PLAY
STOP
REC
OK
MENU

RECORDER

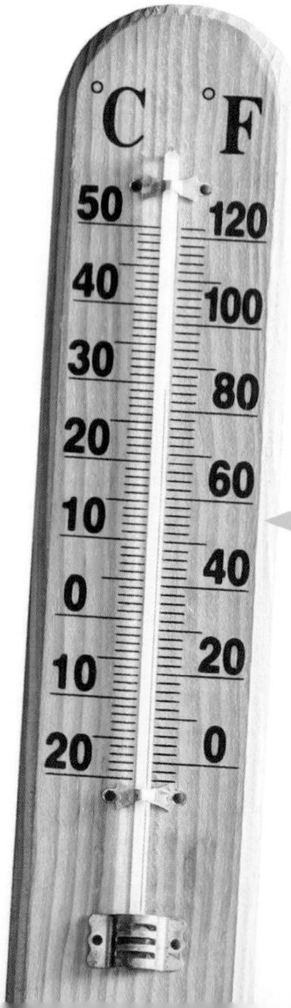
°C
°F
50
40
30
20
10
0
10
20
120
100
80
60
40
20
0

Ghost Hunting Tools

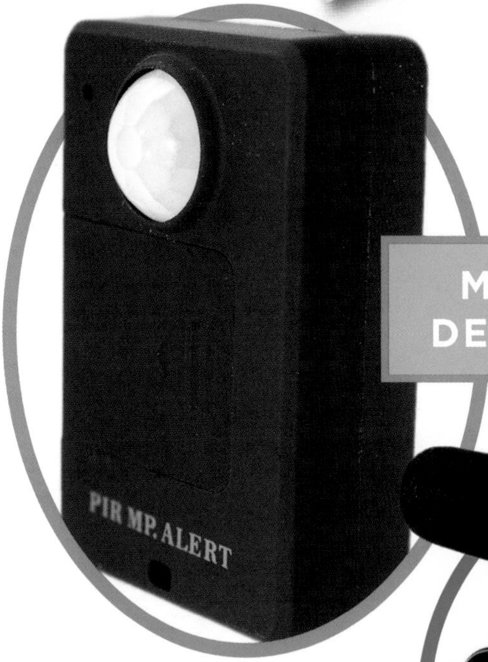
PIR MP. ALERT

MOTION DETECTOR

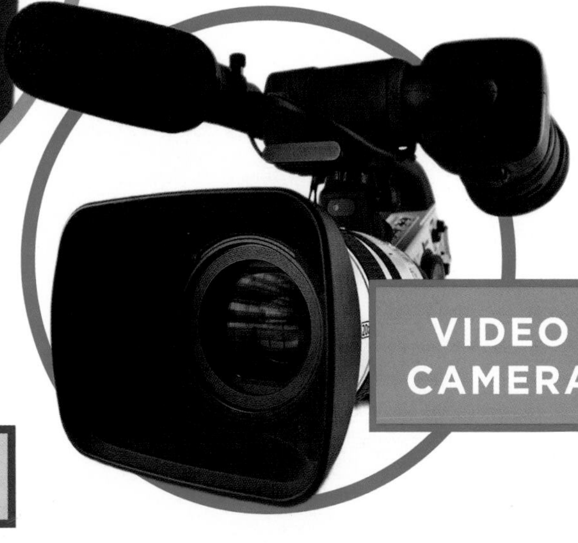

VIDEO CAMERA

THERMOMETER

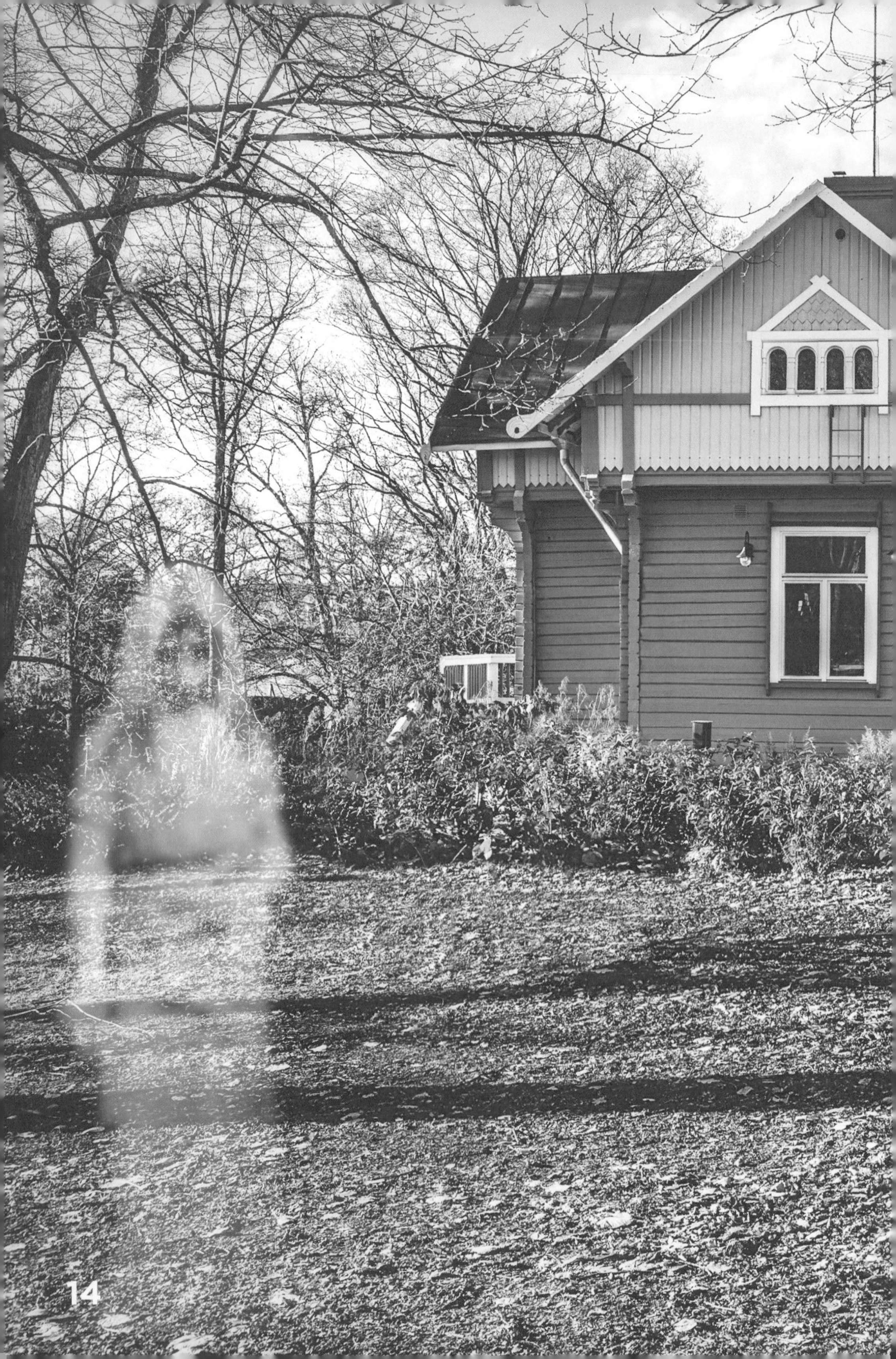

CHAPTER 3

Ghost Stories

In 1994, a boy in Arizona took a **gravestone** from a cemetery. His family used the stone as a doorstop. Soon, strange things started happening. Doors slammed shut. The TV turned on and off.

When the boy put the stone back, the trouble stopped. The family believes a ghost was in their home.

WHAT'S GOING ON?

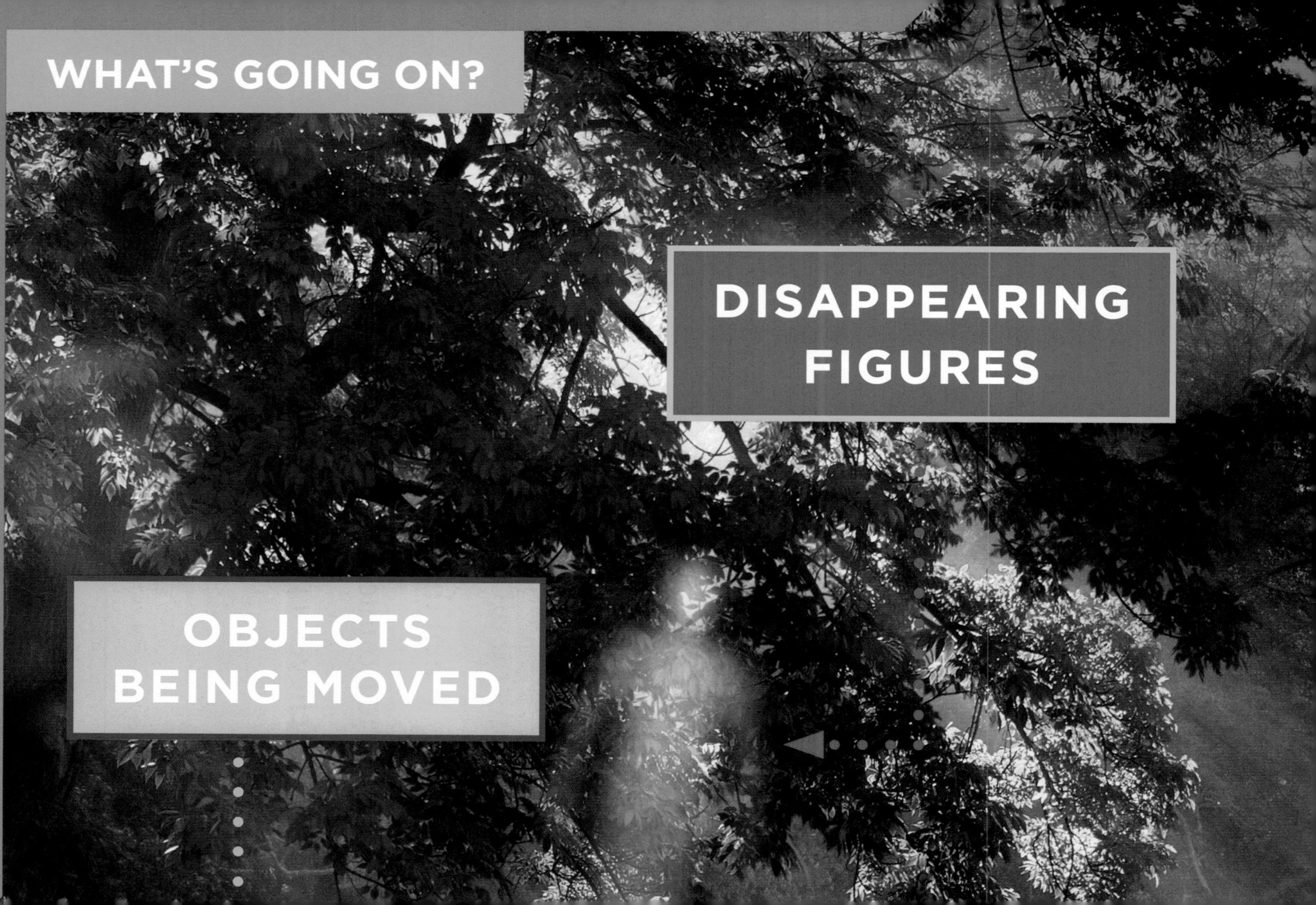
DISAPPEARING FIGURES
OBJECTS BEING MOVED

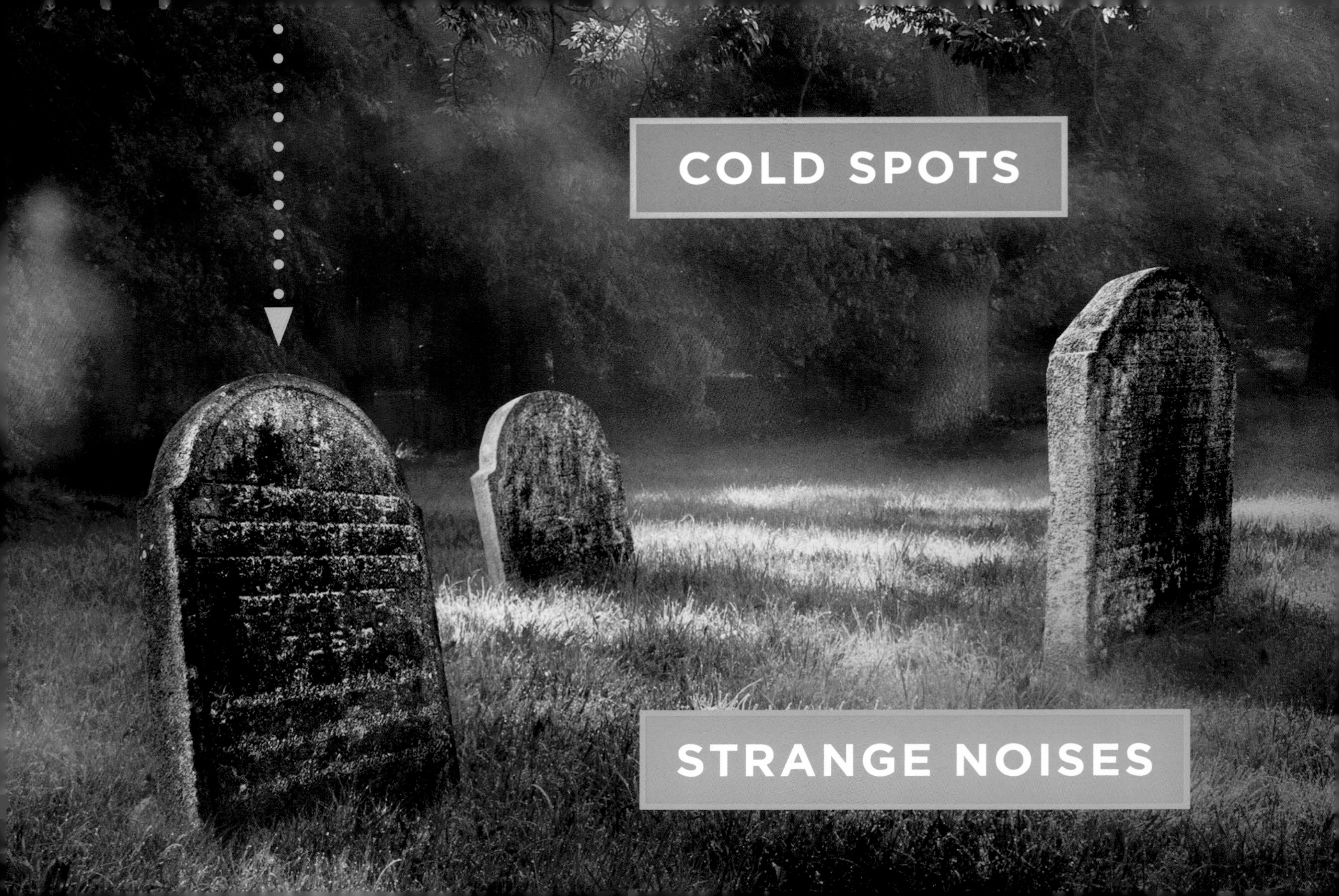
COLD SPOTS
STRANGE NOISES

A Musical Ghost

About 50 years ago, a couple lived in an old house in Toronto, Canada. At night, they heard piano music. Other times, they heard heavy footsteps. They lived in the house for four years. But they couldn't figure out where the noises came from. Finally, they moved out.

Soon, another couple moved in. They heard the same sounds. They moved out in a few weeks!

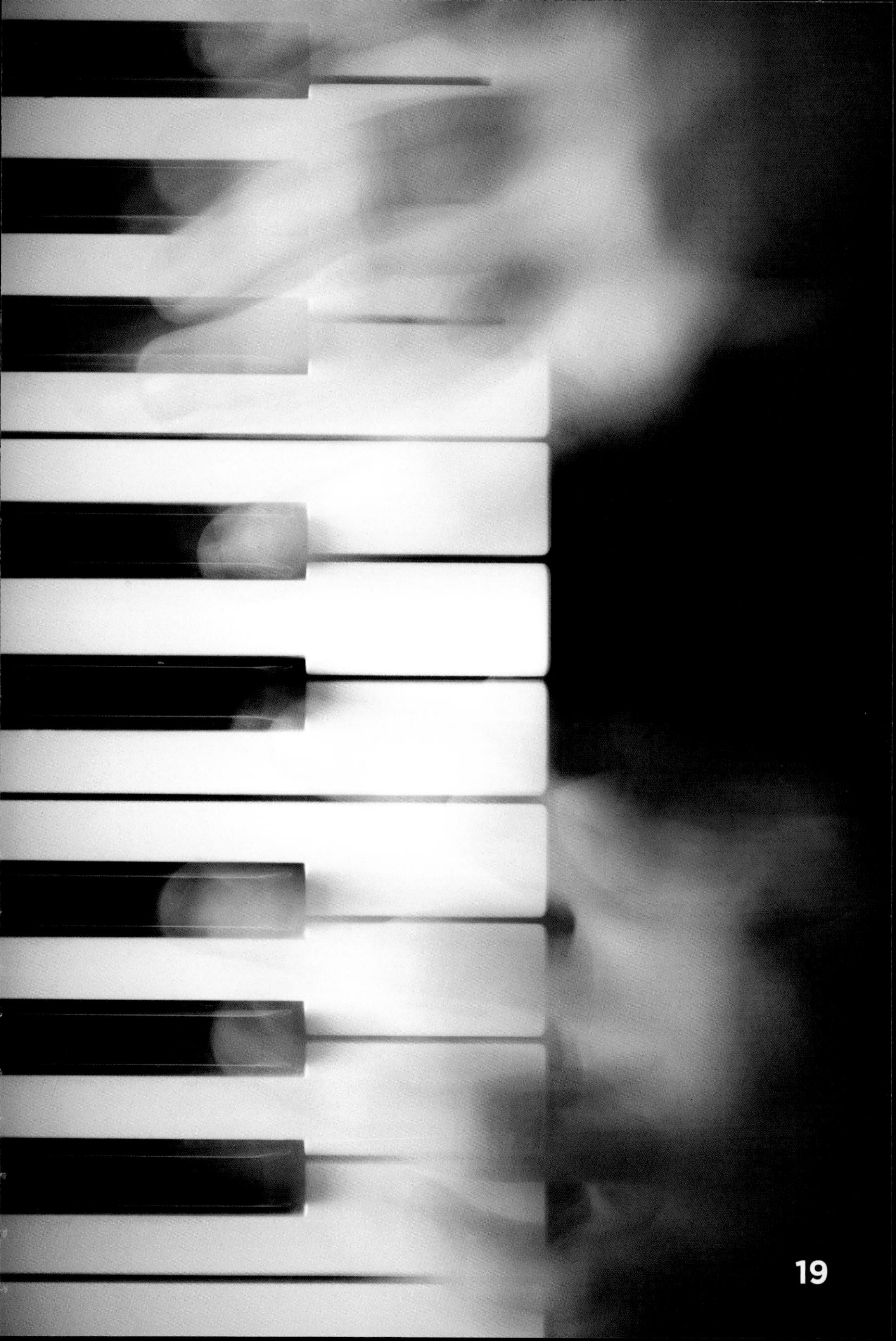

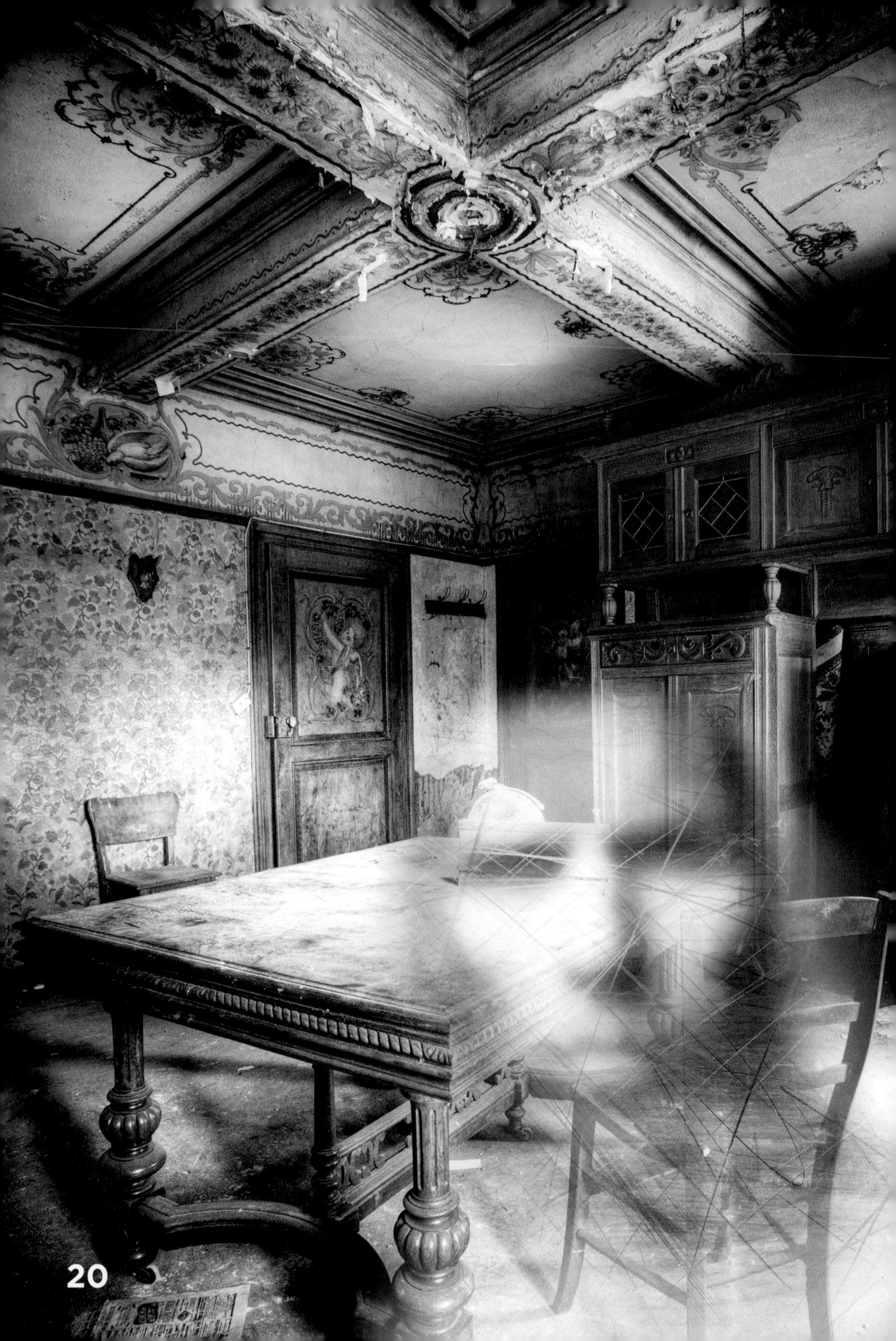

The Reading Ghost

A security guard was working one night. He saw a man carry a book into an office. The guard followed the man into the room. No one was there. But the book was on the desk.

The next morning, the guard learned the man he saw had died. The man died hours before the guard saw him with the book.

The White House is often called the most haunted house in America. People claim to have seen ghosts all over the house.

Ghosts around the World

Stories of ghosts come from all around the world.

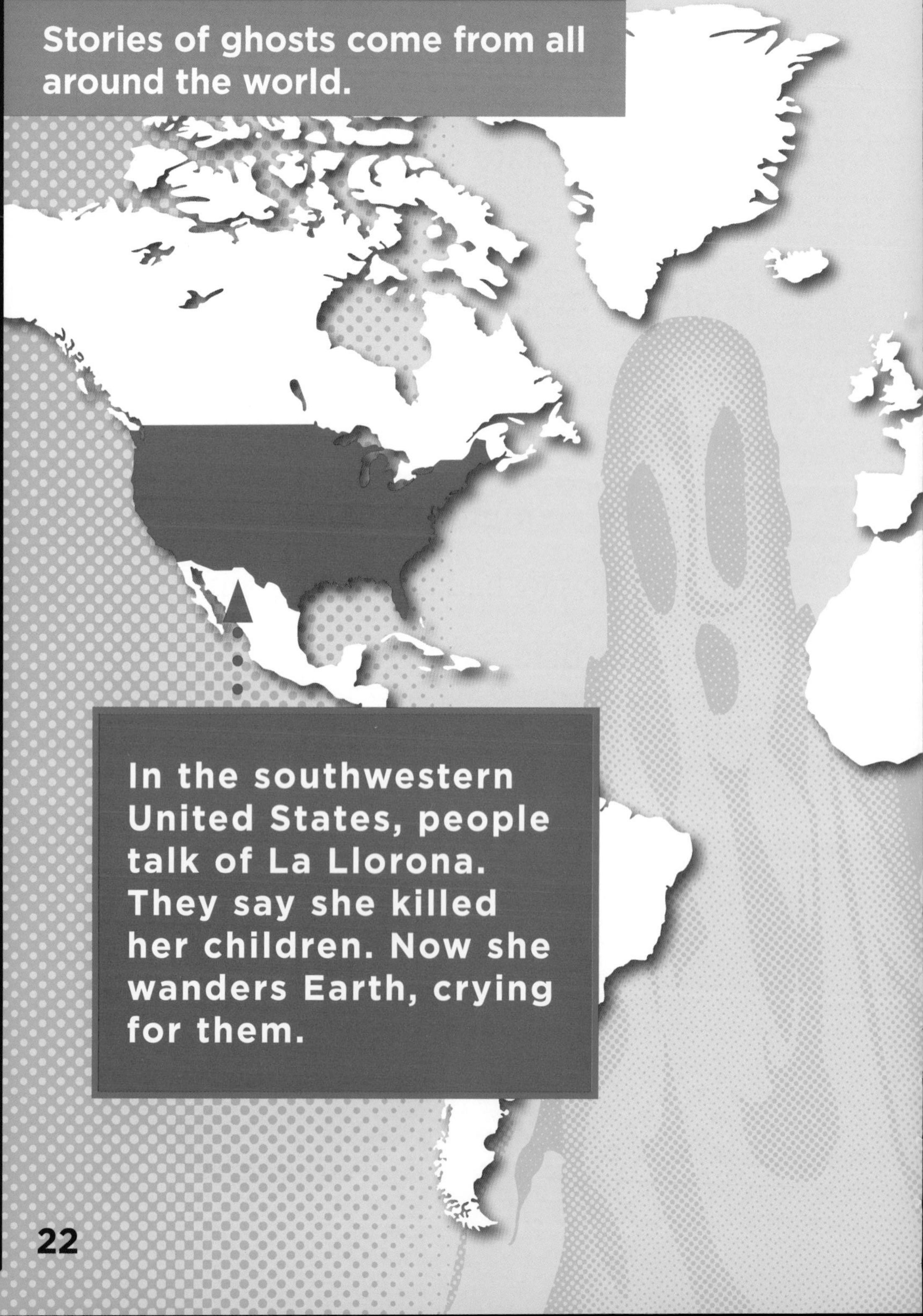

In the southwestern United States, people talk of La Llorona. They say she killed her children. Now she wanders Earth, crying for them.

In Sweden, a silver train is said to carry only ghosts.

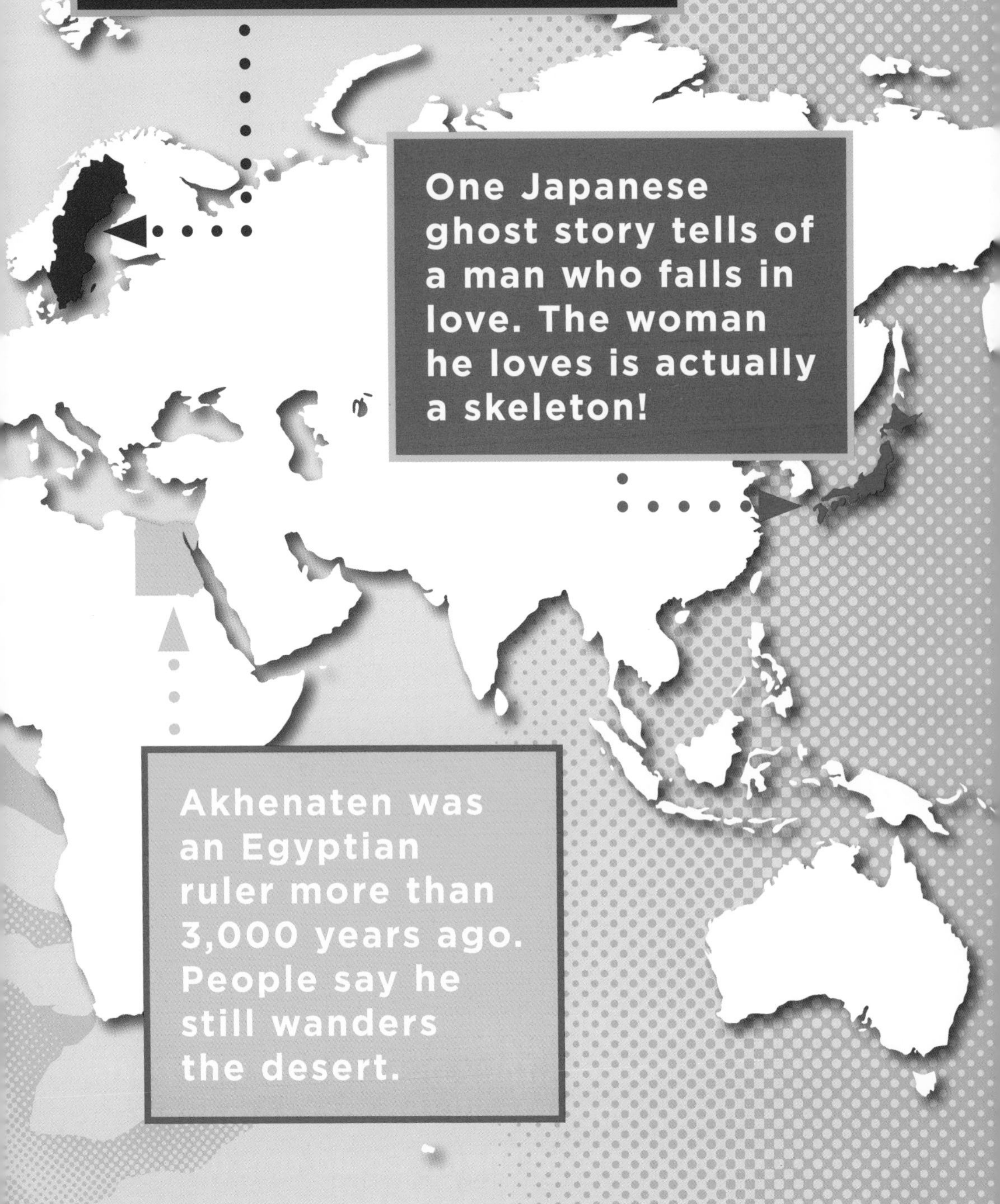

One Japanese ghost story tells of a man who falls in love. The woman he loves is actually a skeleton!

Akhenaten was an Egyptian ruler more than 3,000 years ago. People say he still wanders the desert.

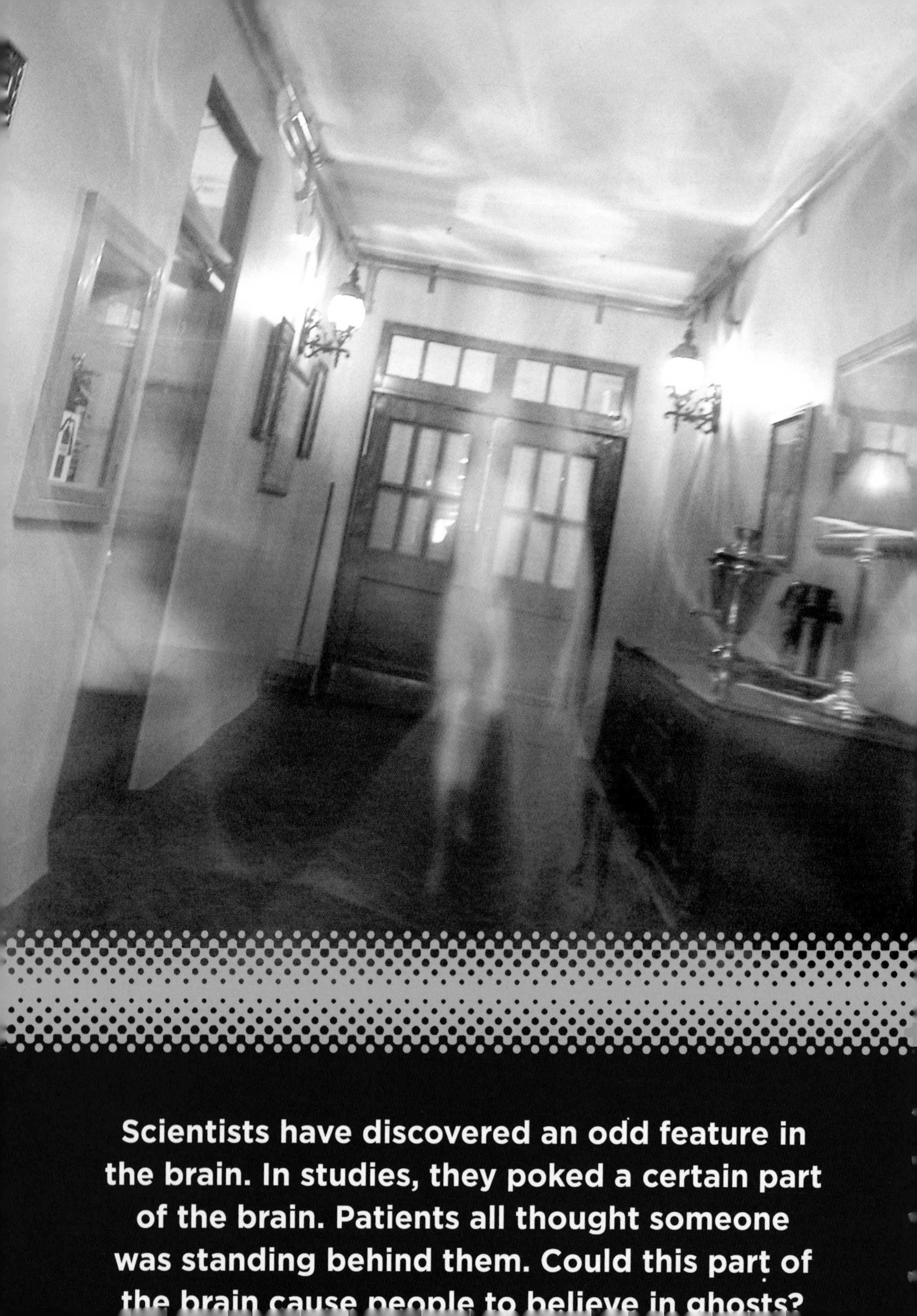

Scientists have discovered an odd feature in the brain. In studies, they poked a certain part of the brain. Patients all thought someone was standing behind them. Could this part of the brain cause people to believe in ghosts?

CHAPTER 4

Searching for Answers

Some people believe they have seen or felt ghosts. Others believe they have seen ghosts in photos. But other people don't believe in ghosts. They say all ghost stories can be explained with simple answers.

Everyday Explanations

Skeptics say strange noises are really ordinary sounds. Maybe an animal made a nest in the home. Bad windows let in cold air. Pictures of ghosts could be blurry photos.

No one has been able to prove ghosts exist. But no one has proven they don't exist, either. What do you think?

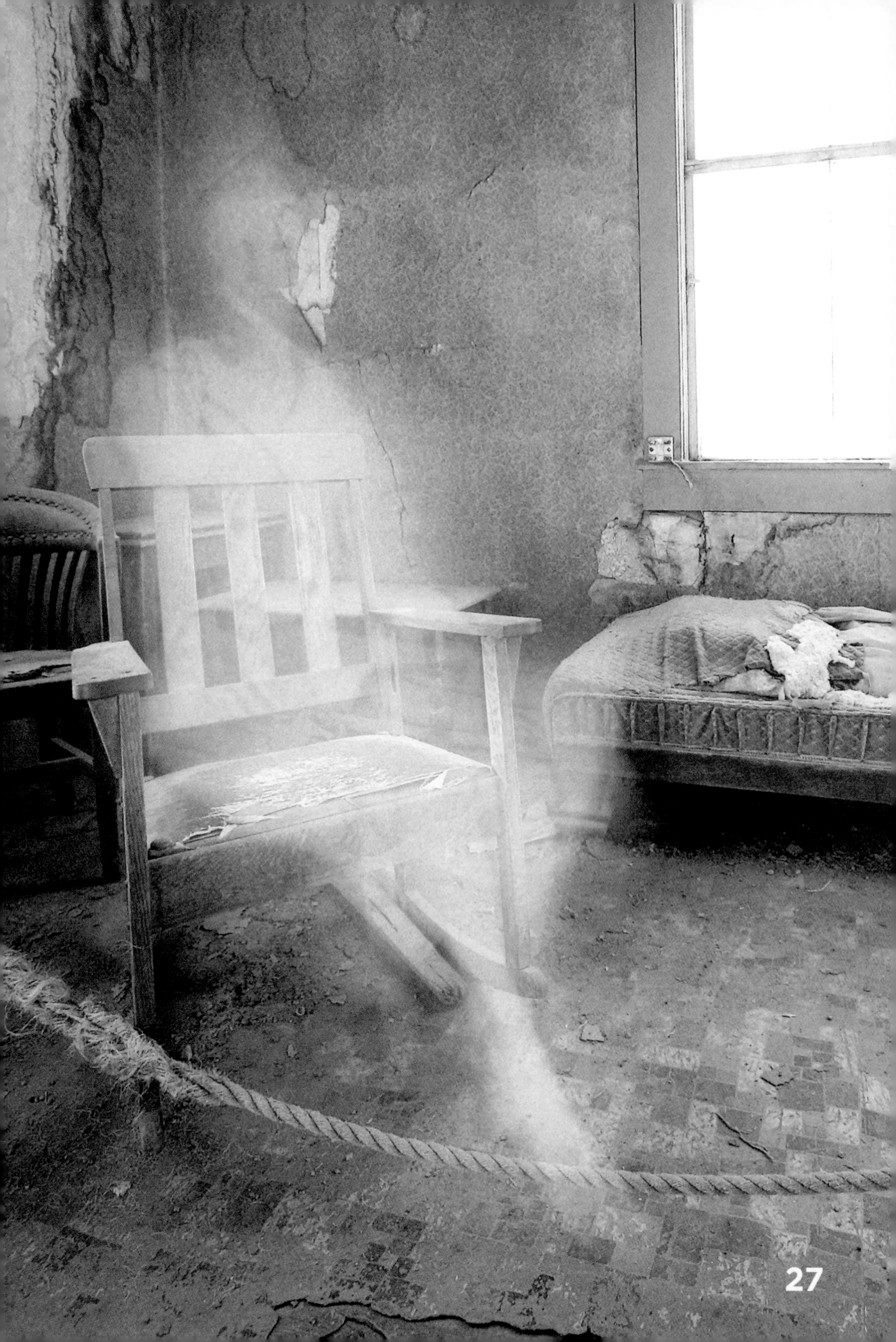

Believe It or Not?

Answer the questions below. Then add up your points to see if you believe.

1 **You jolt awake and see a figure whisk away. What do you do?**

A. Scream! (3 points)

B. Hold the blankets and your breath. (2 points)

C. Roll over and go back to sleep. (1 point)

2 Can a part of the brain make you see things that aren't there?

A. No. My brain knows when something's strange. **(3 points)**

B. Maybe. **(2 points)**

C. Definitely. **(1 point)**

3 You see a door close without anyone around. What do you think?

A. A ghost is definitely doing that! **(3 points)**

B. Weird. I wonder how that happened. **(2 points)**

C. The wind must have blown it shut. **(1 point)**

· · · · · · · · · · · · ·

3 points:
There's no way you think ghosts are real.

4–8 points:
Maybe they're real. But then again, maybe they're not.

9 points:
You're a total believer!

29

cemetery (SEM-uh-ter-ee)—a place where dead people are buried

evidence (EH-vuh-dens)—something that shows something else exists or is true

figure (FI-guhr)—a person or animal that can only be seen as a shape or outline

gravestone (GRAYV-ston)—a stone that marks where a dead person is buried

haunt (HAWNT)—to visit or live in a place; the word is usually used when talking about ghosts.

imagine (i-MAH-jen)—to think or create in your mind

skeptic (SKEP-tik)—a person who questions something

BOOKS

Coddington, Andrew. *Ghosts*. Creatures of Fantasy. New York: Cavendish Square Publishing, 2016.

Frisch, Aaron. *Ghosts*. That's Spooky! Mankato, MN: Creative Paperbacks, 2014.

Perish, Patrick. *Are Ghosts Real?* Unexplained: What's the Evidence? Mankato, MN: Amicus High Interest, 2014.

WEBSITES

Ghosts
sd4kids.skepdic.com/ghosts.html

Introduction to Ghost Investigating
kids.ghostvillage.com/jrghosthunters/index.shtml

Where to Go to Sleep in the World's 10 Scariest Haunted Houses
discoverykids.com/parents/where-to-go-to-sleep-in-the-worlds-10-scariest-haunted-houses/

INDEX